Ellensburg Public Library
Ellensburg, WA 98926

DISCARDED BY THE
ELLENSBURG PUBLIC LIBRARY
ELLENSBURG, WASHINGTON

First published in 1981 by Nord-Süd Verlag
Mönchaltorf and Hamburg
Filmset in Great Britain by Latimer Trend & Company Ltd, Plymouth
Printed in Germany by Druckerei Uhl, Radolfzell
First published in Great Britain in 1981 by Faber and Faber Limited
3 Queen Square London WC1N 3AU
Reprinted 1983
All rights reserved
Illustrations © 1981 Nord-Süd Verlag
English text © 1981 Faber and Faber Ltd

British Library Cataloguing in Publication Data
Nikly, Michelle
The Princess on the nut.
I. Title   II. Claverie, Jean
III. Die Prinzessin auf der Nuss. English
833'.914'J   PZ7
ISBN 0-571-11846-1

THE PRINCESS ON THE NUT

OR THE CURIOUS COURTSHIP OF THE SON OF THE PRINCESS ON THE PEA

by Michelle Nikly
translated by Lucy Meredith
with pictures by Jean Claverie

faber and faber
Nord-Süd

P rince Caspar was no ordinary prince. He was the son of the Princess on the Pea, whose story is told by Hans Andersen. She was so sensitive that one pea under a pile of mattresses was enough to keep her awake all night. This proved she was a true princess, and so a prince who had been searching everywhere for a true princess chose her for his wife.

Time passed. The prince became king, and he and his wife had one son, Prince Caspar. When he was twenty they decided that he was old enough to be married.

"You will have to look hard to find a princess as perfect as your mother," said the king with a sigh. "But there must be one somewhere. It's just a question of finding her."

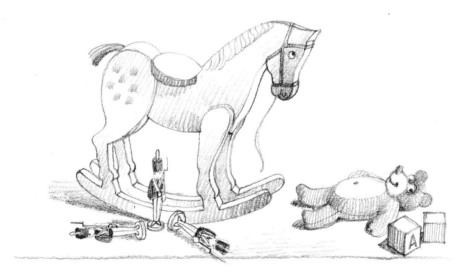

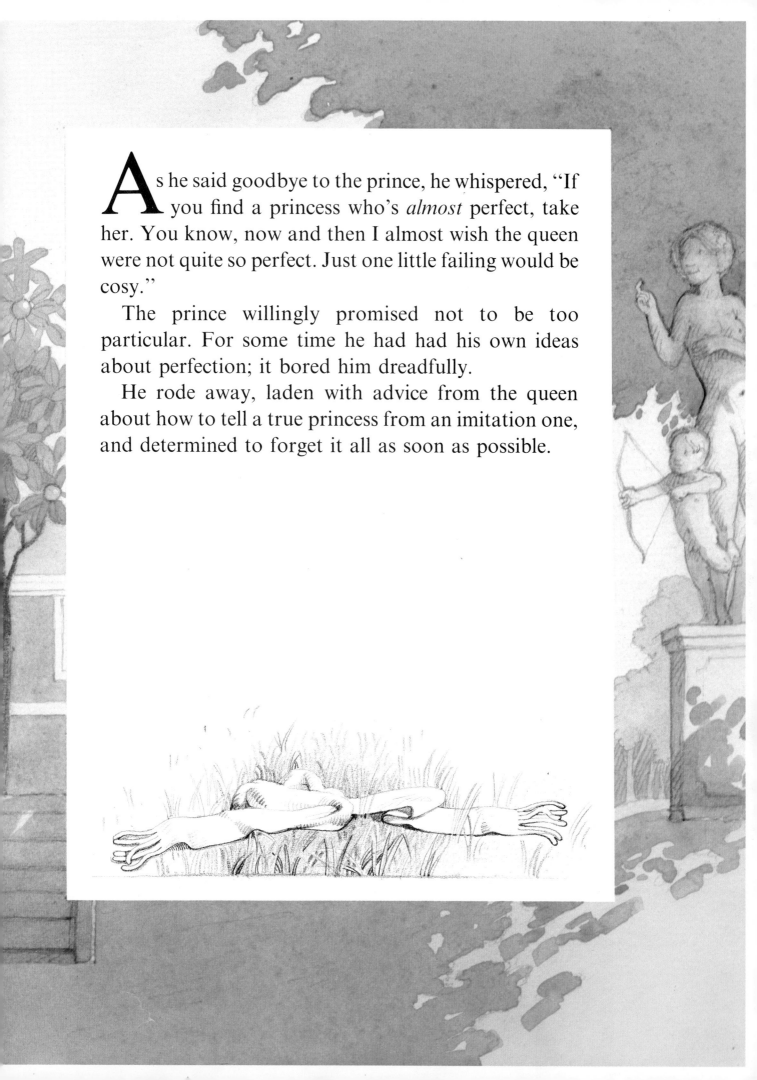

As he said goodbye to the prince, he whispered, "If you find a princess who's *almost* perfect, take her. You know, now and then I almost wish the queen were not quite so perfect. Just one little failing would be cosy."

The prince willingly promised not to be too particular. For some time he had had his own ideas about perfection; it bored him dreadfully.

He rode away, laden with advice from the queen about how to tell a true princess from an imitation one, and determined to forget it all as soon as possible.

He rode for several days, till he came to a foreign land, where he asked the peasants who were working in the fields, "Do you know if there is a marriageable princess in this country?"

"One?" they said. "There are three, Your Highness. And as to marriage, nothing easier. We see more barefoot tramps in these parts than handsome princes like you. Ride to the castle and you can be sure they'll be glad to see you."

The prince rode quickly to the castle, and he was indeed eagerly welcomed by the king and queen.

"I'd be delighted to meet the three princesses," he said as he made his bow.

"Unfortunately there are only two at present, Your Highness," said the king. "Princess Ariana has just left us. The boldfaced thing has got it into her head that she wants to see the world. You can imagine what a disgrace and anxiety this is to us. But we have cast her off, and we think all the more of her sisters Arletta and Arabella."

The princesses were sent for, and very pretty they were. The prince felt his heart beat faster as he greeted them, and he asked if he might spend a day alone with each of them to get to know them better. The king and queen agreed and it was decided that Princess Arletta should spend the next day with him.

When he came to find her she had already been up for hours. She was wearing a voluminous apron and was so hard at work with a feather duster that not even the smallest speck of dust in the furthest corner escaped her. The prince was impressed with the spotless cleanliness of her room.

After housework it was time for cooking. She asked him what he would like to eat and went to work at once. She soon had a delicious meal ready for him, and he greatly enjoyed it. But after lunch Arletta began sewing and the prince began yawning. "This princess is a wonderful housewife," he thought, "but she hasn't much to say for herself."

When he talked about books, music and poetry, she said she had no time for them, she was too busy sewing. By now Caspar was longing for the day to be over, and as soon as he decently could he suggested another meal. Afterwards she began sewing again, and he made an excuse to leave her.

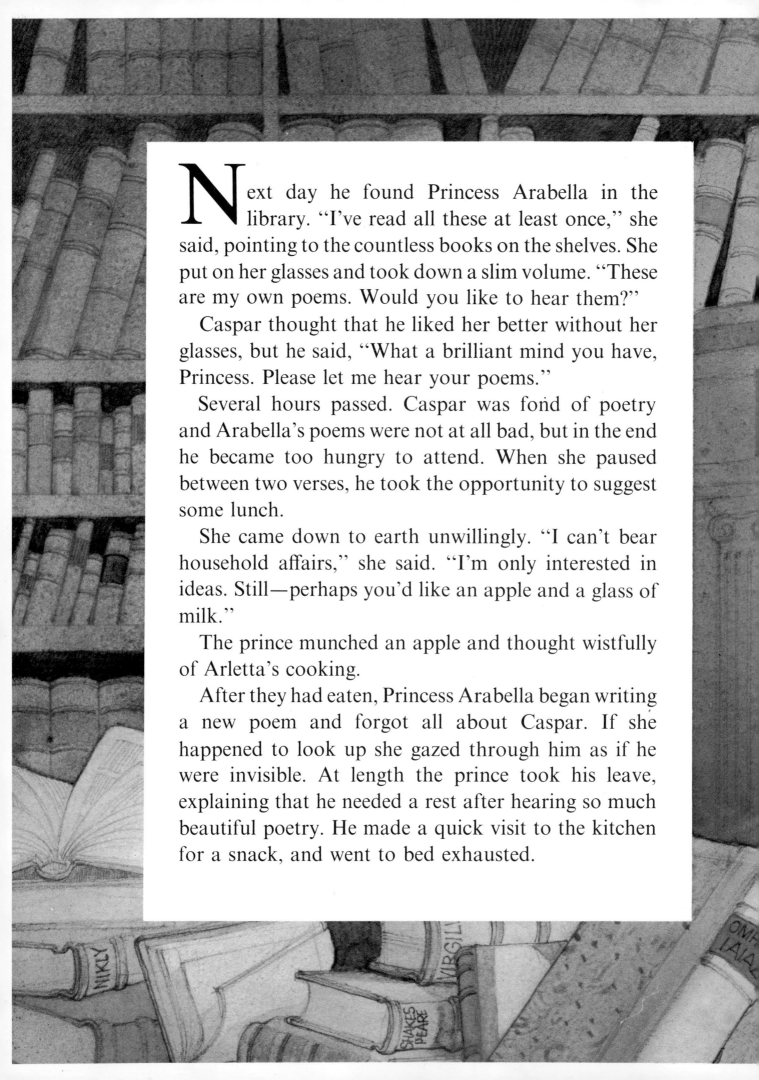

Next day he found Princess Arabella in the library. "I've read all these at least once," she said, pointing to the countless books on the shelves. She put on her glasses and took down a slim volume. "These are my own poems. Would you like to hear them?"

Caspar thought that he liked her better without her glasses, but he said, "What a brilliant mind you have, Princess. Please let me hear your poems."

Several hours passed. Caspar was fond of poetry and Arabella's poems were not at all bad, but in the end he became too hungry to attend. When she paused between two verses, he took the opportunity to suggest some lunch.

She came down to earth unwillingly. "I can't bear household affairs," she said. "I'm only interested in ideas. Still—perhaps you'd like an apple and a glass of milk."

The prince munched an apple and thought wistfully of Arletta's cooking.

After they had eaten, Princess Arabella began writing a new poem and forgot all about Caspar. If she happened to look up she gazed through him as if he were invisible. At length the prince took his leave, explaining that he needed a rest after hearing so much beautiful poetry. He made a quick visit to the kitchen for a snack, and went to bed exhausted.

Next morning he explained to the king and queen that he didn't feel he could make either of the princesses happy, and left as quickly as possible.

He travelled on through the world. He rode through many countries and met many princesses, but none of them really appealed to him.

At last he grew weary of the hopeless search and rode back home, to tell his parents that he had decided not to marry after all. He came to the castle at twilight. It must have been raining heavily, for the path was still running with water and a rainbow was fading in the sunset light.

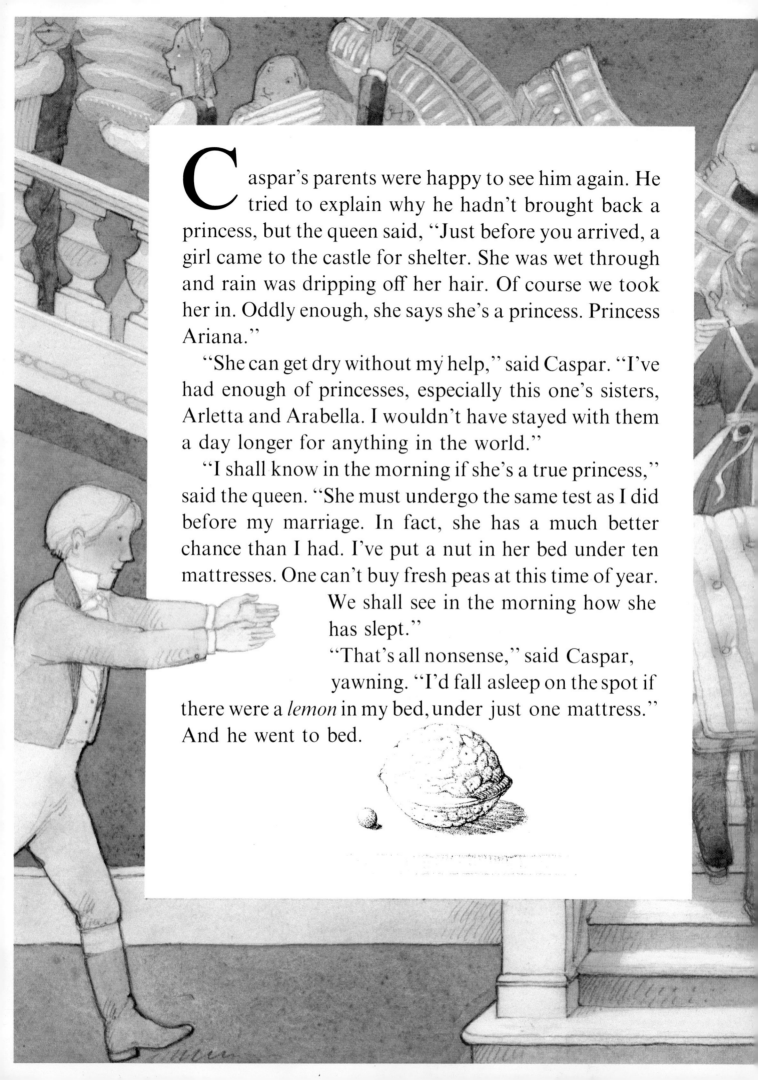

Caspar's parents were happy to see him again. He tried to explain why he hadn't brought back a princess, but the queen said, "Just before you arrived, a girl came to the castle for shelter. She was wet through and rain was dripping off her hair. Of course we took her in. Oddly enough, she says she's a princess. Princess Ariana."

"She can get dry without my help," said Caspar. "I've had enough of princesses, especially this one's sisters, Arletta and Arabella. I wouldn't have stayed with them a day longer for anything in the world."

"I shall know in the morning if she's a true princess," said the queen. "She must undergo the same test as I did before my marriage. In fact, she has a much better chance than I had. I've put a nut in her bed under ten mattresses. One can't buy fresh peas at this time of year. We shall see in the morning how she has slept."

"That's all nonsense," said Caspar, yawning. "I'd fall asleep on the spot if there were a *lemon* in my bed, under just one mattress." And he went to bed.

Next morning the prince was awakened quite nearly by the sound of horses' hoofs. When the queen entered his room she looked bewildered.

"What times we live in! You'd really have thought Princess Ariana was a true princess. But she slept all night like a dormouse. On a nut! When I think how sensitive *I* was at her age... I'm afraid we must give up hope of finding a true princess. Well, she's gone and no loss... a princess seeing the world! It's not proper. In my time..."

The prince had got up quickly. His eyes were shining, but the queen was too much taken up with her lamentations to notice. He hastily said goodbye to his astonished parents and galloped away without a backward look. At the first crossroads he saw a horse. Its rider heard him approaching and looked round.

It was a young girl.
"Princess Ariana," he thought. He hesitated for a moment, remembering her sisters, but somehow he knew that she was quite different from them. He asked her, "Which way are you going, Princess?"

"I was just wondering," she said. "I think I'll take the path through the woods. What do you think, Your Highness?"

"That's the way I was going," he said. "Shall we ride together for a while?"

And their horses went on side by side.

Ellensburg Public Library
Ellensburg, WA 98926